CHEAP JEEP

ISBN 0-89868-360-2–Library Bound
ISBN 0-89868-413-7–Soft Bound
ISBN 0-89868-361-0–Trade

A PREDICTABLE WORD BOOK

CHEAP JEEP

Story by Janie Spaht Gill, Ph.D.
Illustrations by Bob Reese

 ARO PUBLISHING

4

Mr. Wong thought, "My jeep is old. I could buy a new one if this one sold." The sign that hung on the old, worn jeep read, "Jeep for sale, very cheap."

The Browns stopped by to take a peek. "You need to paint this peeling jeep."

So, he painted his jeep like he was told. "That's nice," he thought, "it doesn't look so old."

The Smiths stopped by to take a peek. "You need new tires on this old jeep."

So, he added new tires like he was told. "That's very nice," he thought, "it really doesn't look so old."

The Jones stopped by to take a peek. "You need new seats in this old jeep."

So, he added new seats like he was told. "That's very, very nice," he thought, "it surely doesn't look so old."

The Greens stopped by to take a peek. "You need a new motor in this old jeep."

So, he added a motor like he was told. "That's very, very, very nice," he thought, "it definitely doesn't look so old."

The Cooks stopped by to take a peek. "You need a new top on this old jeep."

So, he added a new top like he was told. "That's very, very, very, very nice," he thought, "it absolutely doesn't look so old."

The Lees came by to take a peek.
"You need more lights on this old
jeep."

So, he added more lights like he was told. "That's very, very, very, very, very, nice," he thought, "now I know it's not so old."

They all came back and took a peek. "You've done a lot to this old jeep.

Now your jeep looks very nice.
We'd like to buy it, just name your
price."

He started the motor and shook his head,

"It's much too nice to sell," he said.

Mr. Wong took off in his fancy jeep,

with a sign on the back, "I fix cars cheap!"